To Louise and Denise

First published 2005 by Walker Books Ltd
87 Vauxhall Walk, London SE11 5HJ

This edition published 2006

2 4 6 8 10 9 7 5 3 1

This book has been typset in Block

Printed in China

British Library Cataloguing in Publication Data:
a catalogue record for this book is available from the British Library

ISBN-13: 978-1-4063-0131-1
ISBN-10: 1-4063-0131-0

www.walkerbooks.co.uk

Potty Poo-Poo Wee-Wee!

Colin McNaughton

WALKER BOOKS
AND SUBSIDIARIES
LONDON · BOSTON · SYDNEY · AUCKLAND

Littlesaurus
did a poo.

"Here's a potty, Littlesaurus,"
said the Daddysaurus.
"What's it for?" said Littlesaurus.
The Daddysaurus told him and
Littlesaurus laughed and
laughed and sang
very loudly,

"Potty POO-POO wee-wee!"

And the Daddysaurus said,
"Shush! It's rude to say it so loud."

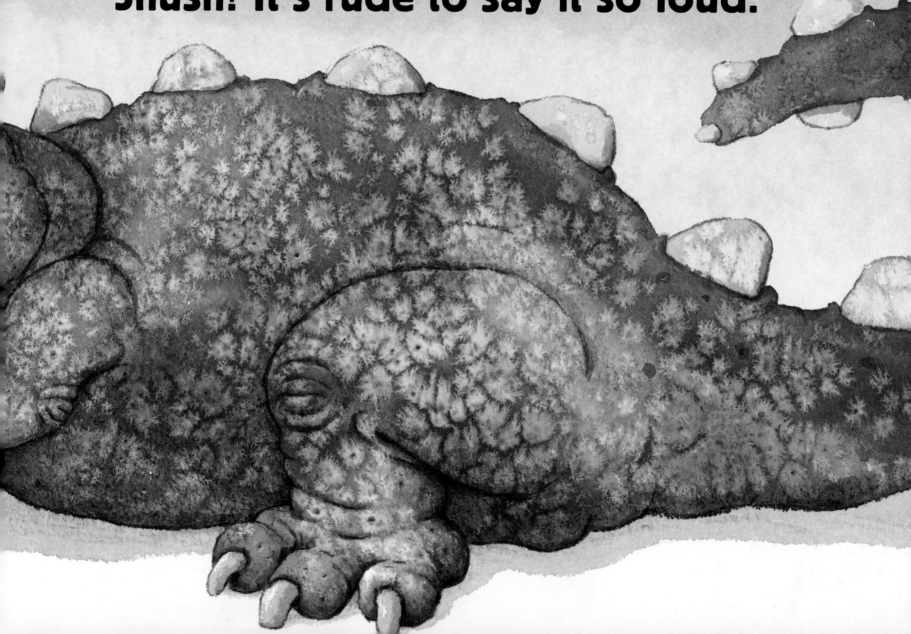

Littlesaurus
did another poo.

"Use the potty, Littlesaurus!"
said the Mummysaurus.

"Potty POO-POO wee-wee!"

sang Littlesaurus very loudly, and the Mummysaurus said, "Shush! That's rude!"

So Littlesaurus DID use the potty. He used it to make sandcastles and sang,

"**potty POO-POO wee-wee!**"

And the Auntiesaurus
said, "That's rude!"

He used it as a hat and sang,

"Potty POO-POO wee-wee!"

And the Unclesaurus said, "That's rude!"

He used it to carry rock cakes
and sang,
"Potty POO-POO wee-wee!"

"That's rude!" said his friend
Whippersnappersaurus.

The Mummysaurus and the Daddysaurus worried that Littlesaurus would NEVER use the potty.

"Don't worry," said the Teachersaurus, "he'll use the potty in his own good time."

"Potty POO-POO wee-wee!"

sang Littlesaurus VERY loudly.

"Shush! That's rude!"
said the Teachersaurus.

"Don't worry," said the Bigsistersaurus, "the more fuss you make, the worse he'll get."

"Potty POO-POO wee-wee!" sang Littlesaurus.

"That's rude!"
said the Bigsistersaurus.

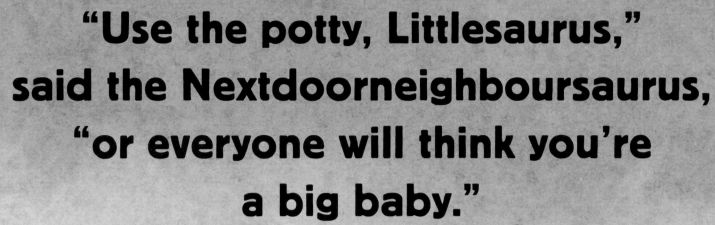

"Use the potty, Littlesaurus,"
said the Nextdoorneighboursaurus,
"or everyone will think you're
a big baby."

"Potty
POO-POO
wee-wee!"

sang Littlesaurus in a big baby voice.
"That's rude!" said the
Nextdoorneighboursaurus.

But the Grannysaurus said,
"Oh, don't you worry
about Littlesaurus.

Daddysaurus was just the same at his age. HE wouldn't use the potty either."

Well, Littlesaurus laughed
and laughed and danced
around singing,

"Potty POO-POO wee-wee

Dad was just the same.

Grannysaurus tolded me,

Dad was just the same."

**And the Daddysaurus,
who was really upset, said,
"I don't care if you NEVER
use the potty, Littlesaurus!"**

"What? Never?"
said Littlesaurus.
"Hmmm …

...I think ...

...I'll use the potty."
And everyone shouted,
"**potty-POO-PO**

And Littlesaurus
said,

"That's rude!"

WALKER BOOKS BY COLIN McNAUGHTON

★ HAVE YOU SEEN WHO'S JUST MOVED IN
NEXT DOOR TO US?
WINNER OF THE KURT MASCHLER AWARD

MAKING FRIENDS WITH FRANKENSTEIN

WISH YOU WERE HERE
(AND I WASN'T)

THERE'S AN AWFUL LOT OF WEIRDOS
IN OUR NEIGHBOURHOOD

WHO'S BEEN SLEEPING IN MY PORRIDGE?

I'M TALKING BIG!

WHEN I GROW UP

WATCH OUT FOR THE GIANT-KILLERS!

HERE COME THE ALIENS!

WHO'S THAT BANGING ON THE CEILING?

★ JOLLY ROGER
WINNER OF THE BRITISH BOOK AWARDS
CHILDREN'S BOOK OF THE YEAR AWARD

CAPTAIN ABDUL'S
PIRATE SCHOOL

CAPTAIN ABDUL'S
LITTLE TREASURE

POTTY POO-POO WEE-WEE!

RED NOSE READERS by ALLAN AHLBERG
illustrated by COLIN McNAUGHTON

JUMPING • PUSH THE DOG • BLOW ME DOWN • LOOK OUT FOR THE SEALS
TELL US A STORY • HELP • ME AND MY FRIEND • BEAR'S BIRTHDAY • HAPPY WORM
SHIRLEY'S SHOPS • BIG BAD PIG • FEE FI FO FUM • CRASH! BANG! WALLOP!
ONE, TWO, FLEA! • SO CAN I • MAKE A FACE